puzzled pieces

matthew j. duncan

Contents

Seattle dreaming.

fill my stomach with Seattle;
wash it down
with the Puget Sound.
pavement pillow,
dense and firm
with the sidewalk at my back.

crown me
the scavenger king
of all the nothing
you've ever seen.

undercurrent of the choir
voices raving,
mumbling,
screaming out for daylight.
quiet streaming
in the techno-city
through electro city

time

shock treatment now.

dumpster diving

—for an Olympic gold—

a degree in difficulty

alongside a BS degree;

keeps me below the freezing

point,

well taken.

move along people—

no tent city allowed.

know tense city

ordinances bury you alive.

can't look me in the facial recognition

staring you back

from your smartphone distraction.

the Morse code language upgrade

chirping at you

is a techno-tongue

i am not privileged to afford…

double shot tall mocha,

with me foaming at the mouth;

no cinnamon.

at the top,

i'm certain you can't see the cost of living

at the bottom of luxury;

on your streets,

and

as your refuse.

at arm's length,

close enough to make you uncomfortable—

but not far enough from sight

to simply fade away.

3

the fourth estate.

propaganda,
pornography of parchment paper—
carnage of hollow words.

not justified—
neither right nor
left in the margins
remain;
the remains of truth.

despondent—
desperate—
marginalized into silence,
stray characters become
well formatted garrison files:
power,
to the fourth estate.

need to know.

decipher understanding—

to find facts in ruin

remain.

implausible,

impossible irrational thought—

an unacknowledged perspective;

the illusion

stretches across a sea of reality.

sanity demands ill-fitting components

of vulgar vocabulary

conform to no logic.

surrender

the need to know.

thought-crime.

i thought crime

thoughtless.

thought,

less crime

begets

civil lives.

civil lies regarded thought-crime—

less chance

and

more circumstance.

perchance,

thoughtless thoughts were somewhere;

where none sense nonsense.

regardless of happenstance

happenings—

some regard thought less
and regard thoughtlessness,
more or less.

regardless of thoughtlessness,
regard less civil lies
less thought;
rather than
civilized thoughtlessness.

work.

insert beautiful blanks
another clip spent;
a full magazine
of empty

hollow pointed eyes—
fixed and dilated.
cardboard cutout targets
to fire upon—
murder is a glamorous art
and glamour is murderous.

goddamn,
the moment is wrong—
roll it back and shoot it again
and again…
another face, another place;
the glamour race—
an untitled roll call of entitled
indistinguishable mannequins…

ok, fine—
people get ready.

well-oiled,
this machine
turning over the media page.
it hums

whimpers
gasps
chokes
vomits
a lifetime of shit sandwiches
force fed to starving mouths—
hungry throats
begging to breath…
so alive.

every day,

the rehearsed lie

was poetry in goddamn motion…

Pavlov's dog could never compete

with the conditioned responses—

until,

a blind eye turned

and well-placed sound

bites the hand

that can't write a check to cover

this work of art

or work in progress?

doesn't matter,

it was just a lot of work.

lessons learned.

thinking
unknown thoughts thoughtlessly;
with no known second thoughts
given.

misgiven consequences
not withstanding
these circumstances unknown
are not thought less understood,
but understood thoughtless
and less understandable…

wrong ways left
behind
are the right ways
to be sideways.
anyways of thinking thoughtfully
left undecided thoughts
decidedly not thought about

corrected action

vs.

incorrect reactions.

out of sequence consequences

correct imperfectly

implausible

impossible circumstance

in possible sequence

unfolds incorrect events

but correct in sequence.

the lessons learned are

thought left over;

leftovers thought

less and less learned,

become lessons learned…

in history.

touch up the edges,

paint a pretty picture;

history

—like god—

is in details

spat from the mouths

of convincing liars.

savior or monster—

your sobriquet

depends upon bodies

beneath your feet

when you stake your claim.

war and spoils,

for god and country

confer immunity and absolution—

it's a package deal.

from survivors' guilt-ridden memories

rationalization—

an exceptional Band-Aid

a bastard called victory.

know salvation is afforded

under the hazy din of a gaslight—

strike a match,

blow up the world.

headlines.

are we making headlines
or at least
the 5 o'clock news?
are we front page bound
or fated to be
buried behind the classifieds—
not noteworthy at all?

no surplus carnage.
nothing sensational;
demanding of a headline.

image or echo,
our short-sighted scope
is always fixated on dark stars.
drawn into negative space;
consigned by curiosity.

so strange,

how black and white the world is

with you so close.

our casual existence

became victim

to this modern crime—

headline attraction.

fall outta heaven

onto the cover of a magazine.

first sight,

the second coming

gonna be first class—

flawless—

all the way.

VIP—

do i look like i wait in line?

jet past the payday people…

razor sharp folded money

tucked into

a double-breasted straight jacket

puts you where everyone wants to be;

caught

in the camera eye contact lens…

that scene;

that's obscene.

everyone's a social critic,

love to post hate;
but at least they know your name…
keeps you trending.

where do you go
for the photo op?
if you aren't the first name listed,
is the photo credit line
worthless…
or priceless?

you're welcome
well, worn out.
look at me…
look at me…
why is everybody looking?

lights…
camera…
reaction…
to what's on the front page.

runway fascism.

baby
understands brand appeal.
the tightly woven national cloth,
custom cut away
imperfections.

leaving an idealized realization
one size fits all...
blinded by brilliance
of the ultimate vanity plate—
a collective of will
masterfully manipulated.

runway fashion—
runaway fascism—
a cost hardly affordable
by anyone's means.
but goddamn,
you'd sell your soul or a million others
to be seen—

to be obscene—

sharp and crisp,
like fresh cut money,
artfully crafted and forced to fit.

so Boss—
shut up!
you will love this
—I SAID—
YOU WILL LOVE THIS.

too perfect;
no need for closer inspection.
design so flawless,
god gets lost in the details.

a seamless transition
from day to evening
—right to left—
without missing

a single goose-step.

a hate couture de force.

a brand of nobody;

demanding "it" without question.

no,

no critical review;

or culling of public opinion.

the sounds you are hostage to—

the echo chamber

of populist unpopular opinion—

a craft of forgery design

no one is buying.

a short journey.

wandering away in-between
places and pieces.

peace is
not found quietly.
it smells like gunshots and
sounds like violence—
it rumbles like a subway train
between stations
compressing rushed hours.
into this human sewage drain,
overfilled to capacity.
i am anonymous.
all the spinning wheels
grind to a halt—
grind us to nothing.
we scurry like rats
on a short journey
over an elaborated distance
in a hell of a hurry.

chaos theory.

wild thought:

multiplied by

(a derivative of the times)/(unknown)

the answer—

non-linear, of course

the hand of man raises

the three-body problem.

resolve,

from consistent variables,

an end result

mostly real and rational

on a linear plane.

indicate the logical designation

in actual terns—

theory this is not.

assume the variables conform to

(basic prime) and (basic prime)—

unreal and irrational;

while differentiated in relational component,

both remain necessary relative factors

nonetheless.

the result should

by minute—

second—

align to a common plane,

undiminished by relative designation.

if the sum of these factors

yields an irrational result,

are inconsistent equations blamed

or

is there perfection

in my chaos theory.

end up.

this was a place
in-between dimensions;
not meant for people or daylight.
but where i always
returned to.

boomerang in full effect.

it belched smoke
from the revolving door,
cycling the undead across its threshold
in perpetual motion.
the walls dripped nicotine,
tobacco and failure.
a pit from where no hope escaped,
the surrender point of the modern world.
no cell reception;
cash only,
no ATM onsite.

fuck, have we actually gone back in time?

a place with communication
still tethered to the wall
and mirrors coated with the residue
of decades;
where we all end up.
attempting to resurrect dreams
after drowning them in a bottle.

fading.

flickering lights—
a faded illusion
scorches my nightmares.
watch
as i raise hell
before you close your eyes
on earth.

skipping my daydreams
across a cesspool
of raw human sewage;
the tide i am swimming against.

am i wasting time
drying off
in the middle of a rainstorm?
your gaze, disapproval—
disappointment—
is all you ever gave me.

are you surprised
that i regard them
as nothing more
than dynamite waiting to explode?

watch me,
break apart this life
like a fortune cookie—

i deserve all the unknown,
not just the crumbs.

fastway nights.

climb into the backseat,
back row…

lights
going down
in the peep show.
watching sound careening;
a drive by—
the fast way is one-way
up a dead-end street.
warning signs overhead
up ahead of a concrete barrier
slamming headfirst into me.

wide awake
a live hotwired memory
stolen in a flash.

just a joyride

going wrong way

down the sunrise highway—

another fugitive racing blindly

into tomorrow.

here is now.

deliberate time pours quickly,

unrestrained—

today is through.

another pitcher of kamikazes… shot down.

numbing the knowledge

somebody poured me into human form

is the what i'm running from.

the distance between

time strangling me…

drowning me…

is a future-to-be time

just out of reach.

a one-way ticket to

any/where

i'm ambling toward.

along the winding road,

this episode of "self-induced amnesia"

out of sync with digital time

is distance between us
like a vacant lot.

...a lot of
distance from you then
to me now....

with time converging.

finally,
here is now
where i want to be.

hey you.

walking by this corner,

waiting on the hour

—it's always happy somewhere—

wasting days away again.

channel surfing,

looking for that moment

to tune back in.

who's gonna sound a warning,

twist my arm;

twist reality

into this prison

been living for years.

treading in water

mixed with whiskey,

chased by second chances.

now i'm sober

and here;

neighbor to a liver on a bar stool.

bartender, come on over—

pour another round.
last call for a lost soul
at the intersection
of hell and too far gone.

a handful of rain
in my bourbon

—or are those tears watering my drink down—
staring at heaven
from the bottom of a glass,
hell is what i found.

imagine amnesia.

Instamatic fate

to be undeveloped memory;

stuffed in a box

forgotten and lost over time.

your hand,

suffocates the world

where i struggle to breath.

drowning in gin

lessens the pain.

2. lesson the pain—

all my person evaporated.

no one noticed as i became subatomic

over the course of their lives.

connect the instances…

sleep to work to whatever,

lather, rinse and repeat;

form and functional survival technique

making sense of senseless existence.

warning signs;

the general observations

regard becoming redundant.

imagine living amnesia.

face to face

with everything you try to avoid;

captured in photo negative proof

of a life never lived.

in wait of wings.

are you able to see?

hear?

summer song

unwound its retreat until gone;

all along the winding road

waved as it faded into a quiet distance.

time,

deeply bronzed and luxurious,

sank sharpened teeth into daylight—

offering only

cold comfort and colder shoulder.

short and somber

seconds of shallow breath passing by;

watching the kaleidoscope tumble down

on our heads,

blanketing the ground in mosaic.

hues of blushed apple red and golden sky-flakes
litter upon tan and emerald walkways—
autumn in a garden lost.

crisp arctic heavens bear witness
to innocence—
creators of earth-bound angels
attempting to leap from ground to glory.

never believing themselves
to be the angels in wait of wings,
but the restraints—
inseparable chains,
keeping them from heaven.

nonsense and nothing.

is the only way to save myself
running away;
each mile,
one step at a time?

are you high right now?

dripping sweat—
tasting sin
with the boys who didn't call
and the little white lies
which used to be truth.

now, it's every day.

every time i get my ATM receipt,
wondering:
will i pay rent this month???
i need to be high.

how can i contemplate rehab?

drugs are my comfort.

i want to laugh at misery

fucked up next to you.

to build a house on crack pipe dreams—

drown in gin and tonic—

dance until moonlight dies—

fuck in a k-hole—

let's kill each other away.

i never knew hell could feel like heaven;

damage taste so sweet.

high is never enough

wandering the 3am world

talking about nonsense and nothing—

me and you.

order in cuisine.

starved by luxury—
prisoners willfully ignorant,
wither away their illusion;
the appearance of status.

all the internet porn
and point and click convenience
of a throw away generation—
on-demand,
and easily forgotten.
is it wrong?
probably.

but
left in the wake of this vanity
desperate for affection,
they are all they have.

honesty raped—
a trade negotiation of survival.

timid emotion and unblemished skin;
in the hierarchy of needs,
are disposable.
discarded scraps in the trash,
like remnants of takeout/
order in cuisine.

fuck,
everything can't be seen in that moment;
when we empty ourselves
to our base ego.

consume all their details
in a familiar ritual of one-night stands
on filthy mattresses.

wipe the taste from your lips
with a trembling hand,
before spitting
a barely audible goodbye on the floor.

was it all you had imagined,
unfortunate rag doll;
the touching and attentions
on twisted sheets?
is this the why
you grew up so fast—
the guilt of love kept secret,
screaming into a pillow
wishing to be invisible—
to be nothing
anyone desired.

real time pornography.

our now found cell phones

map a course taken

—previously unknown—

of flesh and adrenaline.

behind camouflage,

the unseen primitive of nature.

undercurrents;

urge driven and driven urgently

by technology.

stop action images

taste of salt

dripping off temples,

abbreviated machine gun breathing

accompanies being obscene

and unseen

with you.

is there sense or rationale

feeding senseless irrational hunger—

or just the chemical ignition

of skin on skin?

in the instant of confusion;

oh wait,

your name was what?

impatience is footnoted

in our breath on fogged glass;

signed with smeared fingerprints.

documentation from the backseat

where

i fell in lust with you.

undercurrent forecast.

joyous is priceless;
the cost of misery, bankruptcy.
i keep throwing blank checks
into a wishing well—
see what i'm wishing for…

together,
we're unpredictable.
never know whether
i'm up against stormy weather.
no forecasting
to let me know
if you're gonna change
the direction you're going in
or blowing the other way.

just waiting on whether
you'll just tell me

if you're meeting me halfway?
pushed up against your storm front,
wondering if my breaking point
will lead some other way?
an event horizon
before the curtain calling,
nighttime falling
down around us—

i continually not see
the hell raining down on me.

midnight blues,
in the air
from everywhere;
out of nowhere

hand grasping fading notes,
no words are written…
downstairs

a sleeping angel—
—little monster
stares.

tell me,
what it is you see
looking down at me?

am i someone else
in nobody's dream?
trapped in the reflection
you're holding up,
holding me down.

daydreams of going nowhere

or where

nightmares are waiting

past my fingertips,

just out of reach.

lips moist in fear,

savoring a taste

of an unknown

is what i'm wishing for.

hook upgrade.

your bio-metric interface
in my face…

pay for play—
foreplay,
is your FORTRAN tongue whispering
bytes across my T1 line.

by the minute…
buy the minute…

my service as a service
isn't open source…
a limited time trial offer.

if you want this hook up-grade
plan beyond
world wide web borders;
my SMS 140 characters
is exclusive to you.

why chat online—
in public IRC where icu2?
let's direct connect
c2c in a private room…
without a million voyeurs
hacked into a pay per view,

paid by you.

…what the font?
do you like it BOLD or
is it better when i'm italicized?

are my keystrokes
getting through to you?

on command,
pick the image for your system—
personalize your personal
virtual obsession.

i'll materialize

your material lies,

i'm turning it on for you.

train wreck.

beautiful,
violent and vulgar—
train-wreck of emotion in motion
stepping out of graffiti.

rising from
pools on the pavement,
a trash can rhythm section
keeps the time;
a well squandered score
knee deep in sky high.

won't you be blues with me?

chasing stars crushed by gravity
before they begin to non-exist.

i noticed.

subtle is the shotgun in my mouth;
transparent as atmosphere-
i'm all wrapped up

in black and blue,
present to be
unwrapped—
yet again.

things the mind already knows.

familiar,

family man-dated

outdated;

demanding

demeaning

the meaning ....

who we are.

aren't you worthy?

deserving?

serving desire—

not out of the blue

or

left field—

but,

by right of entitlement

or

by rite of blood, sweat

and please don't…

cry me a river.

no helping hand.

swept away

everything you know.

know,

the hand that rocks the cradle

rules the world—

ruins the world.

because,

any cause justified,

pure and simply right

left,

right,

left behind

childhood dreams.

childish dreams overpower

to the people—

by the people—

buy the people,

all the things

the mind already knows.

commuter rush.

attention on the platform,
the evening commuter
is currently derailed…
thank you for your patience.

i am not waiting
with this platform
of a cross vivisection of society,
meat puppets waiting to be devoured.
all outstanding
of sound and reason.

i hear
hopes and dreams
shattering on the sidewalk.

i am overdone.

the gridlock of bodies competing for space.
the frenzy
of being left on the platform;
like children playing party games,
desperate not to be odd man out.
to be part of the mass
arriving at the appointed destination
behind schedule.

i dislike constraints of time;
a dictation without merit
and inefficient.

should i arrive,
in my own incremental meandering;
it will be awash in sound and
gorging on vice.

emoji.

thought about texting you,

"good morning,

i can't sleep"

only to remember

i am no longer part

of your good mornings.

but i can't sleep,

and you don't do relationships.

can't text feelings

—letters or emoji—

formats leaving a lot to be desired

in the wake of

uncommunicated silence.

i need

the back and forth argument.

the strife of an immediate eternity,

not enduring the endless procession

of you blasting the alphabet
from an unknown location.

don't matter
if you blow up my phone
faster than 5G streams…

it lacks the betrayal
of the look on your face
when you won't look me in the eye.

damn,
do you even know how to talk to a person—
not at their number?

who knows,
we could still be staring at the same problems.
'cause i'm right here
in the same room as you,
not half a world away.

Instagram moment.

twilight
slowly saturating the tangerine sky,
cloaks shy carnivores
in eager pursuit of
America's litter.

playing hide and seek
or
catch and release—
unremarkable games in forgotten alleys—
back roads—
back rooms
where innocence is gambled away.

left or lost,
but not found out.
flirting girls photocopy
magazine cutout images

meant for g.i. joe boys
pretending to be men.

both grown too soon…

dull present tense presents
this unfortunate technicolor picture show
of reality now.

gunmetal grey whistles aimlessly
turns to thunder.

I-2 Nowhere…
can't miss that exit.

a lightning flash assures

this perfect Instagram moment

will be pasted and posted—

feeds and photo streams

overflow the internet ocean;

a net tangled around everywhere.

an anchor drowns moments

in the depths of eternity—

always on

always online

life untethered.

zero to talk about it—

this wasting time;
a wasted life untethered.
my contact high
drifts away with the details;
into a bland background
lacking imagination.

everything
plain beyond explanation.

choke down reality
faster than its force fed,
like a never-ending last meal.
sorry,
no substitutions allowed.

if this is the road to nowhere,
at least it's a scenic route.
i was beginning to wonder
to wander

lust for my dreams.
a life far and away
from this path beaten down over generations.

we are all shoved
into the oncoming 8 lanes
of everyone else's expectations;
scrambling to find ever-after.
past the propaganda
of god, mom and American pie—
where our toe-tag
hasn't devalued these lives
before they are begun.

Mass Ave.

blankly,
through stained glass eyes—
at the filthy pavement,
god stares.

from font to sewer,
sin flows freely—
evolution washed away
the debris of our creator.

in holy daylight,
the hallowed house welcomes
god's children…
human misery follows
the decay of faith—
the empty promises of hope
descend.

there is no salvation,
no sanctuary here.

behind glass ignorance,
see her crouch in the shallow nave—
wrapped in rags and yesterday's news.
bitter rain
threatens her shallow grave

found at god's feet,
in his plain sight,
she suffers—
the hand of grace falls.

messiah.

dark streets full of people,
this overpopulated parking lot
is waiting on a messiah—
exiting a convenience store.
waiting for salvation
to come along;
easy as crossing the dimensions
of a common doorframe.
drinking divinity
from a brown paper bag;
waiting on the express line,
to be on time.

look through his stained glass eyes.
his daylight vision
melts into the sea at night;
staring through me
and stumbling into my open grave.
a freshly dug abbreviated space
in-between purgatory and hell;

asleep in dirt and concrete

sky beneath my feet,

memories drift through my fingers—

stretched into nothing.

sorry.

is a single word

a thousand miles long;

deep as a shot glass.

in a graveyard of empty bottles

and

empty crucifixion hypodermics

where i ended

before i began.

in the dynamite jet saloon.

ignite

a hole in a son

from the back of the moon—

watching a universe decay

away.

a half-life spent

half thinking

about the meaning of

undone and empty

down the sewer drain.

under the street

light a match…

a chain reactionary

sets

motion in reverse.

obsidian sludge

scraped off the asphalt,

jumps from the pavement—
hell's angels
raised to the glorious heaven.

whimpering thunder
and flickering lightning bolt
of blue
returns to the gun,
holstered

enjoying the sale
of day old doughnuts
and stale coffee—
amidst the machine gun chatter
of voices…

of those undead
at the crack of o'dark AM,
again.

moonlight peering in

through the bulletproof glass—

watching the violence,

hearing no sound,

mindless…

…mind you;

here,

the sound of a pound

on the door,

on the floor…

against all odds,

another day

is set into motion.

gods blind eye.

is god watching or
blinded;
blind sided
by all he sees?

did no one notice
or even see
he who lived in plain sight—
a plain life,
invisible.

in visible sight of blind eyes,
he was more than crumpled paper
or discarded rags.
it was his crumbling remains
locked in eternity
that drew attention.
their morning cup of routine
delayed—

all eyes were upon him,

waiting...

until the OCME ushers

paid him their respective service—

unnamed acknowledgement.

normal is reset.

daily grinding and pressing;

man to vagabond to unknown.

the dirge-like pipe organ

and hell's choir screaming

until—

coffee bleeds out for the masses.

he

becomes the topic of discussion

for the waiting line.

the #hisnameunknown
becomes the focus for this week's outrage.
their fixation on this everyday fault
of everyone but me
until the next shiny social injustice
takes over social media
and public attention.

until then,
lip prayer service
is paid in memorial
to the he no-one bothered to know.

what was his name?

carefully constructed care packages
to bandage the open guilt wounds,
a visible and vocal damning
of the appointed social consciousness—
for their own benefit.

there will be rallies

punctually attended and reported

—did you see my picture?

i was there—

and

well paid volunteers

coordinate his burial,

marked by the blank gravestone.

and as in his life,

the search for his name

will fade away.

mosaic of blues.

New Orleans

wailed and howled in my ears

painted blues on my soul—

not lonely notes

saturated in bourbon and agony

but brilliant brass notes

from the Treme to Algiers.

Yankee boy swimming in Southern comfort.

a sinner

floating in an ocean of vice.

Holy Cross shone down on me,

no judgement under the crescent moon.

the mambo beat

played loose and wild

magic from fingertips ignites

dense grey overcast

into a neon flood.

hear the call
swing rhythm and ragtime everywhere
drenching all who wander
but are not lost—
found comfort and silence
in a mosaic of blues.

a vanishing scene.

it wasn't until i stopped
that i heard what you had said.
it's funny how "i love you '
sounds just like "goodbye" to me

it looks like everything is falling away.
the man i thought i had become
is dying a little faster—
every word you say
is the joke killing me.

i guess that i was never
a part of you
and you were everything to me;
you left in such precision,
i barely heard the slam of a door.

instead of a supernova
punctuating the end of a life sentence
between you and then,

an inaudible yawn barely rippled the space

for a few more moments—

a vanishing scene before closed eyes.

the look of disaster in human form

without a filter to mask the face—

look at me looking at you

before you backed away.

bayou soul.

bayou soul
draped in moss—
tears large as a crocodile,
quiet as nighttime,
sleeping between the cypress trees;
barely over the cemetery's shoulder
and
two steps from the move.

a voodoo heart
beneath a full moon rises—
rhythm unchained begins.
razor blades of grass
slice the breeze to whistles and shrieks;
iridescent dragonflies dancing across the remains of
a day.
grasping for the neck,
predator and prey deeply entwined.

a sonic boom shattering silence
levels high walls to low ground.
glistening with sweat,
shadows splattered in muddy finger-paints emerge;
born
for this lunar moment.

time,
an hourglass without end,
extends its hands of hours and minutes;
a thousand miles of bayou long.
everyone come,
rattle moonlight—no one hears;
frenetic until daybreak sentences
a frantic return to slumber.

divine thing.

hop,

skip,

jump over here—

cross walk reality…

be my divine thing.

dance lunacy with me;

until lights out—

blackout

dependent state amnesia

comes to my rescue.

clawing at the ceiling

and

pressed against

reality

flattening me into non-existence.

the floor
bored with me,
like a glass half empty—
but i am half fulfilled.

a world of words
tumbling from my mouth—
don't you hear me?

shake, shake, shake some action
rattle the door
and pound down
the stares
i am attempting to escape.

graveyard.

this graveyard of empty bottles

is an obvious statement—

no matter how hard i try,

i can't drown you out.

why is it every fuckin thing i see

somehow brings you back to me?

i never wanted you,

but we wound up

decimating each other's lives.

it seemed apparent,

how inadequacy

was the only part of me

measuring up to your estimation.

still,

my automatic actions

were ultimately our undoing.

all you did was push buttons.

over there,
in the furthest corner of my damage
are scraps of amnesia—
of the time we killed together.
deconstructing
the heavy awkward

an insistence of this moment—
the familiar uncomfortable of being with you.

you returned
a non-event of soulless flesh.
so,
the open grave beside me
i invite you to fill.

hangover reflection.

summer's lazy and elongated

evening temperature still set on toast

embrace my pillow—nightmares to come

morning's chill on the window pane

rub the sleep from eyes half awake

daylight daze on its way

empty bottles

once full of bravado

litter from another night

don't have to pretend anymore

drunk and such a superstar

i don't sense the flooding

ocean through my veins

every sound is melody

whole wide world just drifts away

to heaven from hell

where am i?

torn and confused

between indulgence and excess.

mambo.

shhh, shhh

hands and eyes cast down.

practiced and solemn

are the hands of civilized men

with parchment thoughts

conscripting

fashion of the times

"igbo olodumare"

whispers the land

pound, pound

the ground wakes

rustles alive

skin reacts to the rhythm

and wide eyes giggle

learning to begin

again

so different from before

tahli,

soft skin whispers

behind your ear

the caress of a mother tongue

kisses her children

as spring breeze is gentle.

the fingers that reach

but hold back from

the devil's fork

lodged in the back of their throat

are the hands of young man.

but mambo is coming

hands raised to daylight

before the dusk rolls in

the dusk of childish days

eyes shining bright

there is more than juju can contain

these are the mouths that sing and cry

mambo,

a storm rising

a story coming

a mother calling out into time

madman's song.

an old man in the corner

smoking all the time,

reminder that

bourbon's a whole lot cheaper

during the graveyard of happy hour.

helps keep it all out of focus—

blues in the distance;

notes,

floating behind.

unbalanced scales

of neither word spoken,

while i hold my breath

like an elevator door.

burn down this world,

so you can read

what i've written—

you piece together meaning

as if it were alphabet soup.

but floating with the ice in your drink

and

pills that chase reality away,

deftly hidden in a madman's song

truth defies the reasons

your mind ought to know.

valentine's day.

so tantalizing—
getting trapped
in the tangible lie
of this greeting card moment.
a love-ish story;
eye catching in satin shiny
sold early to the eager.

your touch sends an electric pulse
to disrupt the senses
i trusted.
only god and money
have ever held someone so close.

this is the reason—
why we shatter ourselves.
fractured,
desperately attempting to become whole
filling empty spaces
with someone else's pieces.

maybe,

love is not a cherub

binding people together with heartstrings.

it calculates—

a stalker from behind

the eyes of every stranger;

targets in its cross-hairs.

sentenced to live wide awake.

alert for subtle tells left behind

and too late discovered.

only after

bullets from his devoted gun

hit its intended target

does clarity return…

to find true love's desire

bleeding out on the pavement.

bootblack.

kneel—
match strike in a dark corner,
my wordless consent
given to you.

this silent conversation between
deity and devotee;
a tug of war—
your eyes and mine.

hungry spectators
devour the articulated movements
of my flesh
beneath the red light
meat packing district.

my smeared fingertips dip,
stain,
caress,

worship at the feet
of the craven idol in the chair.
the actions of service are regarded,
consumed—

and settled
as you cross my palm
for fealty.

in that instant,
your dominion is lost.

my eyes and thoughts wanderlust
wander lost once again
for flesh,
fire and spit.
i am on my knees
a god rising.

deep river reflections.

placid surface moments
brew rippling infinity,
the ocean's breath screams—
i strain to hear the destination.
choppy speech
waves to distant shoreline;
the seas thunderous clap
shakes skeletons
balanced on the surface tension:
a forgotten gravesite.

in the depths of calm
cold resolves to find no light.
from canals, sounds and
reaching inlets do become
bays—
threshold to majestic oceans.
inescapable is their grasp

with vengeance deeper than

the river i carved

in my grandparents yard.

resting place of a paper cup boat—

a Water Rat sank into silt,

on an event horizon

beyond reach.

this is how we should say goodbye.

before you,
i was destroying myself
without particular design—
unhappily satisfied
knowing success in life—
the ending of it,
would be mine.

but now,
i want your love.
the free-fall
from a 30th floor window
is how you take my breath away.
why is hitting the pavement
at 100mph less hurt
then hearing "i love you"?
why getting lost in thought
always returns me to you,
i'll never know.

i bring drugs,

you bring pain—

we are cruel to each other

in the way our love is.

together, we are quiet.

survival

is a round-way ticket to anywhere;

i can't be without you.

you are the best and worst

i cling to for hope.

please,

whisper i love you in my ear—

then throw me in front of a train

after you fuck me.

this is how we should say goodbye.

stolen alphabet.

a tapestry in blinding white light
singed at the edges
steal the words from out my mouth
before my gated tongue
reacts

i'm following you too.
these wide eyes shock treatment now—
my stolen alphabet
ready for consumption
alive with thoughts
gracefully sliding into your ears
down your never ending throat
in search of you.

there's more where they come from

hell's not hot
but this scorched universe is microscopic
for both of us to be trapped in
retreat from a caress of frigid fingers
and a frozen french kiss...
it's just business baby
ain't no pleasure with you

just the everyday way of ordinary
numbing us down
dumbing us down...
it's just A, B, C and 1, 2, 3
survival in the world of you.

drop me.

find me in between
gravity and indigo—
roasting in the electric city.
snap, crackle and ka-boom.
plug in,
hotwired to the streetlight—
i need to be alive again.

is the empty crack violent pavement
reverberating "go down moses"
or am i just imagining?
laughing at the small pieces
of reality—
the now-ish and then
is stretched across awake.
convulsing to the bassline,
this assault and battery on my senses
is making perfect sense.
inhale ambition,
enough to sit up and yawn

before falling down…

stares again?

there are no faces—

a barrage of voices breaks my bones;

a battering ram linking past and present.

salvage garbage

—unforgettable and unforgivable—

becomes decompressed amnesia.

i can't leave me alone…

go…

get away…

blow me up 'til there ain't no air to breathe.

let me crash into real time,

until the pieces put back together

reflect this broken lifetime

no one wants to steal.

www.ingramcontent.com/pod-product-compliance
Lightning Source LLC
Chambersburg PA
CBHW070634130626

46555CB00006B/2544